Secrets of
the Matterhorn

Penn Mullin

High Noon Books
Novato, California

Secrets of the Matterhorn

Penn Mullin
AR B.L.: 2.8
Points: 1.0   UG

Cover Design and Interior Illustrations: Damon Rarey

Copyright ©1994, by High Noon Books, 20 Commercial Blvd., Novato, CA 94949-6191. All rights reserved. Printed in the United States of America. No part of this publication may be reproduced, stored in a retrieval system, or transmitted, in any form or by any means, electronic, mechanical photocopying, recording or otherwise, without the prior written permission of the publisher.

International Standard Book Number: 0-87879-979-6

9 8 7 6 5 4 3 2
2 1 0 9 8 7 6 5 4

Contents

All aboard! Justin, Juan, Amy, Miss Lake and Lisa.

It was a wonderful surprise for the four seventh graders in Miss Lake's class when they learned they had won a trip around the United States for their essays on "What Do You Like Best About Being an American?"

Then a mysterious "Mrs. X" read about them in the newspaper. She was so proud of them that she surprised them with an all-expenses-paid trip through Europe with their teacher!

Mrs. X has arranged a surprise for the group in each place they visit. But there is a catch. The surprise can be found only if the kids follow Mrs. X's clues. And the clues lead them to exciting famous places. Even finding their guide at the start of each trip is a mystery to be solved.

CHAPTER 1

Welcome to Zermatt!

"The clue says, 'To find your guide, open at four o'clock – 15 minutes before you get to the Zermatt train station!' It's time!" Amy tore open a long white envelope. She read:

Get off the train, then look for me.

In a carriage I will be.

My hair is red; my hat is blue,

And I can't wait to welcome you.

"This sounds easy! There are not a lot of Swiss people with red hair," laughed Amy.

"And we get to ride in a carriage!" Lisa said. "Far out!"

"Sounds neat. But I feel sorry for the poor horse! We've got a lot of stuff for him to carry," said Juan.

"Justin's backpack is so heavy with all that Swiss chocolate inside!" laughed Amy.

Justin looked out of the train window. "It's really steep out there," he said. "These are *high* mountains!"

"I'm sure glad Mrs. X sent us to Switzerland!" Juan said.

"Whose turn is it to write her a postcard?" Miss Lake asked.

"Mine," Amy said. "I'll send one with a

picture of the Matterhorn on it."

"How far up the Matterhorn can we go?" Lisa asked.

"I think our guide has a great hike planned. Wait and see," said Miss Lake.

"Do they speak French in this part of Switzerland?" Amy asked.

"Yes. You will hear German and Italian, too. These three languages are the main ones spoken in Switzerland," their teacher told them. "But people here speak English a lot, too."

"Geneva was a beautiful city," Lisa said. "I loved its huge lake."

"It is the center of culture in Switzerland," said Miss Lake. "The way Zurich (Zurick) is the

3

center for business."

"I like getting away from the cities," Justin said. "These mountains are the best."

"Hey, I think the train's slowing down! We're coming into Zermatt!" Amy cried.

"Look at all the carriages waiting," Justin said. "We'll never find ours!"

"Start looking for redheads!" laughed Miss Lake. "But get all your stuff together first. Backpacks, everybody?"

The kids followed their teacher off the train. The little station was crowded with people. Bells from the waiting carriages tinkled gaily.

"I don't see any cars here!" said Juan.

"Weird!"

"Zermatt does not allow them," Miss Lake said. "This helps keep it a mountain village!"

"I want to see the Matterhorn!" Lisa said. "I thought we would just get off the train and see it. But all we can see is houses and people!"

"Let's find our guide!" Amy said. "I'm ready to give the horse my backpack!"

"Are you looking for me?" The voice came down to them from a high carriage. Red hair and a blue hat went with the voice!

A tall, smiling young man jumped down from the carriage. He took off his hat and shook hands with everybody.

"Welcome to Zermatt! I am Kurt Wesel.

5

Madame X asked me to be your special guide here. We are going to have a wonderful time!" Kurt spoke in perfect English. "Let's load your things and go to your hotel."

They all helped Kurt pack the carriage. Then they climbed in and started off.

The narrow streets were filled with carriages, electric carts, and people.

"Kurt, we want to see the Matterhorn!" Lisa said. "It's supposed to be right up above us!"

"It is! You will see it in just a moment," Kurt told them. "Wait until we come around this corner. Then look up!"

Just then the carriage turned a corner. The

The Matterhorn

houses were not so tall on this street.

"Now!" Kurt said. "There she is!"

They all looked up at the jagged white peak high above them in the sunlight.

"Wow!" Justin whistled. "It just doesn't look real. Like it's painted up there."

"How high is the Matterhorn?" Miss Lake asked.

"It is 4,478 meters, or 14,700 feet," Kurt answered.

"I can't believe anybody could ever climb to the top of that," Lisa whispered.

"Many people do every year," Kurt said slowly. "But many people die trying, too."

CHAPTER 2

Under the Matterhorn

"Who was the first person who ever climbed the Matterhorn?" Justin asked Kurt.

"A 25-year-old Englishman named Edward Whymper," their guide said. "That was back in 1865. He led a group of seven men to the top. But on the way down their rope broke. Four of the men died."

"That sends chills down my back," Amy said. "Was Whymper on the rope that broke?"

"No, he lived. And he left a diary. We can

read about what happened on their climb," Kurt said.

"I'd like to see that diary," said Juan.

"I have a copy you can see," Kurt told him. "I study it a lot. You see, I want to climb the mountain myself! Next month. That is, if my grandfather thinks I am ready!"

"Your grandfather?" asked Lisa.

"Yes, he has climbed the mountain many times," Kurt said. "He has been teaching me for a long time. And he will go with me."

"Wow! You're going to climb the Matterhorn next month?" Justin asked.

"Yes, before the winter snows come," Kurt said.

"Aren't you a little scared?" Amy asked.

"Yes. I would be a fool not to be scared. But I think I am ready now. My grandfather has taught me well," said Kurt.

"Will we get to meet your grandfather?" Justin asked.

"Yes, he owns the hut where we will stay tomorrow night," their guide said.

"Hut?" asked Amy. "We're going to stay in a hut?"

Kurt laughed. "I guess in America a hut is not a good thing. But here it means a small inn for hikers in the mountains."

"So we get to go on a hike tomorrow?" Juan asked.

"Yes, but I will not tell you where," said Kurt. "You must follow your clues!"

They stopped in front of a pretty wooden building that had boxes full of red flowers at all the windows.

"Here we are! The Alpenhof – your hotel!" Kurt jumped down from the carriage.

"Wow! This place looks neat!" said Juan.

"Come in!" said Kurt. "And bring your bags. Here, Miss Lake, I'll carry yours!"

They all followed Kurt and their teacher into the hotel.

"Welcome to the Alpenhof!" A blond, rosy-cheeked lady met them inside. "I am Marta. Madame X has told us all about you! We are supposed to take good care of you and feed you well!"

"Sounds good to me!" laughed Justin.

"We are very glad to be here!" Miss Lake said. Then she told Marta all the kids' names.

"I love your dress," Lisa told Marta.

The woman was wearing a black velvet jumper with a bright red apron. A crisp white cotton blouse went under the jumper.

"Thank you! This is called a *dirndl* (derndel). It is our national costume in Switzerland," Marta said. "And they are for sale here in Zermat. You can take one home!"

"I hope I have enough money left," said Lisa. "I would love to buy one."

"How could you fit another thing in your suitcase?" Justin laughed. "It is about to pop!"

"Some other things are about to pop, too!" Lisa told him. "Just keep eating your Swiss chocolate and you'll see!"

"Everything tastes good in Switzerland!" Kurt said. "Come on! I will help take your bags to your rooms. Follow me."

They went up the old narrow stairway. Marta proudly opened the windows in each room to show off the view.

"We've got balconies!" cried Amy. "This is something else!" She stood there and looked up at the Matterhorn.

"We've got a clue!" yelled Justin and Juan

from the next room. "Come and see it!"

Everybody hurried into their room. Juan had a piece of paper spread out on the bed. "O.K., here goes!" He read:

Climbers seven in '65,

Three of them were left alive,

Honor the four who fell that day

A tiny church gate will show the way!

CHAPTER 3

The Clue in the Graveyard

"A graveyard! That's the clue! I'm sure it is!" cried Amy.

"There can't be too many in this little town," Justin said. "Let's check a map."

"Or maybe Kurt knows," said Lisa.

Kurt smiled mysteriously. "I know nothing. But I do have a map of Zermatt."

He pulled a map out of his pocket and gave it to the kids.

"There sure are a lot of churches here! This

may take a long time!" Justin said.

"Read the small print at each church," Miss Lake said. "That may tell you if the Whymper group is buried there."

"Yes! Here it is! I found it," Amy said. "Kurt, is this church far from here?"

"No, very close. We can walk there any time you're ready!" their guide said.

"I think there's time before dinner," Miss Lake said. "Let's go!"

"Which way, Kurt?" the kids asked at the front door.

"Look at your map! Can't help. Strict orders from Madame X!" Kurt laughed.

"We take this street," Lisa said. "See, it

goes right to the church! Come on!"

They all took off after Lisa. Soon they came to an old wooden church almost hidden in the tall pine trees.

"The clue said 'a tiny gate.' I wonder if it's this one," Lisa said.

They slowly opened the old iron gate into the little graveyard by the church.

"Now we have to find Whymper's group. This has got to be the place," Justin said.

They wandered around the little graveyard looking at the old headstones.

Suddenly Lisa shouted, "Here! I found them!" Then her voice dropped to a whisper. "They're all together right here."

Everybody gathered around the graves. Justin slowly read off the names of the four climbers: "Hudson, Croz, Hadow, and Douglas, July 14, 1865."

"This sure makes you have a lot of respect for the Matterhorn," Juan said.

They looked up to where they could see the peak of the Matterhorn through the trees. It looked very high and far away.

"How far up on the mountain will we go?" Amy asked Kurt. "Will we be in the snow?"

"No, not that far. We will stay on trails through pastures just below the snow," Kurt said. "That's where my grandfather's hut is."

"Our clues will tell us what trails to take,

right?" Lisa asked.

"That's right," Kurt said. "And I think you have forgotten that there is a clue nearby right now!"

"But where could it be in this graveyard?" Lisa asked. "Kurt, can't you give us a hint?"

Kurt only smiled. "Madame X told me you are very smart."

"The gate! I bet it's there and we never saw it!" Amy said. "The clue told us to go through the gate." They ran back towards the front of the graveyard.

"But it's not here!" Juan said as they searched.

"Wait! I think I see something white! It's

under the gate!" Lisa knelt and tugged until the envelope was in her hand.

"Open it! Open it!" the kids yelled.

Lisa tore open the envelope and read:

Tonight at dinner, order please

A special dish that's made with cheese,

Take your forks and go ahead,

But just watch out: don't drop your bread!

"Cheese fondue! That's what we order to find our next clue!" Justin said. "And I'm starved. Let's head for the hotel!"

CHAPTER 4

Cheese Fondue!

"Welcome to our dining room!" Maria led the way to a big round table.

All the waitresses wore bright-colored dirndls like Marta's. The tables were covered with sparkling white cloths. Bowls of mountain wildflowers sat in the middle of each.

"Look – a band!" Juan said as they sat down at their table. Just then accordian music filled the room. Another of the men played a violin, the other a trumpet.

"I love this music!" Miss Lake said.

Just then Marta came to their table. "Well, what would you like to start off with tonight?" she asked.

"Cheese fondue!" Justin said.

"I thought you might order that!" Marta laughed. "O.K. Fondue with six forks!"

"Fondue is a very special dish in our country," Kurt said. "The cheese they use is so good. You'll see!"

"Do you think our next clue will be in the fondue pot?" asked Justin.

"I hope not! The note said not to drop our bread. So what happens if we do?" asked Lisa.

"You have to kiss all the boys at your

"Here you are, fondue for six," Marta said.

table," Kurt laughed.

"Help!" said Amy. "I'm going to be careful!"

"The same thing happens if a boy drops his bread," Kurt said. "He kisses the girls!"

"Let's forget the fondue," Juan said.

"Oh, you have to have fondue in Zermatt! And remember – there's a big hike tomorrow! So you need to eat well tonight!" said Kurt.

"Here you are, fondue for six!" Marta said. She set a large steaming pot of melted cheese on the table. Next came a basket of bread cubes and six long pointed forks.

"Oh, boy!" said Justin. "Does this look good!" He quickly speared a piece of bread with his fork and stuck it into the pot.

"Careful, Justin. Is that bread on tightly?" Miss Lake asked.

But the bread was already in Justin's mouth. "No problem," he mumbled happily.

Soon all the forks were dipping into the pot.

The band sang some songs in German and Kurt joined in.

"How many languages can you speak?" Amy asked him.

"Oh, let's see. German, of course. And French, Italian, English. That's it!" he said.

"Wow! That's enough!" Justin said.

"Well, Switzerland sits right in the middle

of four different countries. We have France on the west. Italy to the south. Austria to the east and Germany to the north. So we must know their languages!" Kurt said.

Suddenly Juan said, "I almost forgot! We should be looking for our clue! It sure isn't in the fondue pot."

"Let's look on the table. Maybe the clue is under somebody's glass," Amy said.

They all looked under their glasses and plates. But no clue!

"The clue said to order fondue. We did that, so where's our clue?" Juan asked.

"Justin, why are you staring at my fork?" Lisa asked.

"Look! There's something white tucked into the handle of yours!" Justin said.

Lisa looked closely at her fork. "You're right!" She slowly pulled out a tiny rolled up piece of paper.

"Hey! Good work, Justin!" Juan said.

"Here, Justin. You get to read this. You're the one who saw the clue," said Lisa.

Justin unrolled the little paper. Then he read:

Put on your boots,

Take the path to Zmutt,

The footbridge of wood,

Holds your clue to the hut!

"This sounds neat!" said Juan. "How early

can we leave tomorrow?"

"It is a long hike," Kurt said. "So we will start early. Keep your backpacks light!"

"Juan! Look at your fork," Lisa said.

"Your bread fell off!" laughed Justin.

"Time for me to go pack," Lisa said.

"Me, too!" Amy pushed back her chair.

"Now, wait, girls! You can't leave!" Kurt laughed. "It's an old Swiss rule: You can't leave the fondue pot while there's still cheese in it. You don't want bad luck on the mountain, do you?"

"Help!" groaned Lisa and Amy.

CHAPTER 5

The Clue to the Hut

"Does everybody have a water bottle?" Kurt asked. "It's going to be hot today!"

"We're ready!" Justin said. "And we found the trail to Zmutt on our map."

"Your backpack looks really heavy, Justin," Lisa said. "Chocolate?"

"Ha ha. Just wait till you're hungry on the trail. You'll come begging," Justin said.

"O.K. Lead the way to the trail, kids," said Miss Lake. "Time to go!"

They all left the hotel and started up a small side street. Soon they had left the town behind and started up into the high grassy meadows.

"Here's a sign for Zmutt!" Juan said. "So far so good!"

Lots of older couples were hiking up the trail, too. They all wore shorts, long wool socks, and green wool *loden* (loden) hats.

"Those guys are *fast*!" Justin said as one couple zoomed past.

"Wait till you meet my grandfather!" Kurt said. "He is amazing!"

The trail was getting steeper now, and there were far fewer trees.

"Look up there," Kurt said. "You can see the Zmutt glacier. It is a huge mass of ice that slowly flows down the mountain."

"It has a blue color to it!" Amy said.

"Kind of creepy that it's moving all the time," said Juan. "Has one ever come down and covered a town?"

"No, they melt before they get down that low," Kurt said. "But never walk on one. They have deep *crevasses* in them. These are cracks that go way down deep into the ice."

"Are we going to hike near any glaciers?" Amy asked. "I hope not!"

"Near, but not *on*! Don't worry," Kurt said. "How is everybody doing? Are you tired? We are up pretty high now."

"Time for lunch yet?" Justin asked.

"We'll stop soon at the village of Zmutt," Kurt said. "Then you'll have a beautiful view of the Matterhorn."

They hiked up on the trail. There were fewer and fewer other people now.

Finally Kurt called out, "There is the village! Let's have our lunch on this side of it by that big rock."

"Ah, it feels good to sit down," Lisa said. "My pack was getting heavy."

"Mine too! I think Marta packed me an extra big lunch," Justin said. "Oh, boy, look at these sandwiches!"

"I want to see if there are any climbers up on the Matterhorn," Juan said. He took a pair of binoculars from his pack.

Kurt pointed up at the peak. "Look just along that front edge. I think I see some black dots crossing that snowfield."

"Yes! I see them. They're people!" Juan shouted. "I counted five. Wow, Kurt you saw them without binoculars!"

"I have been looking at the mountain for a long time," Kurt laughed.

"Just think. Soon that will be you up there with your grandfather," Miss Lake said. "Is that the trail you will use to climb it?"

"Yes, that's the one. I can't wait!" he said.

"I think I see a footbridge!" Justin yelled.

When lunch was over they walked through the tiny village of Zmutt. Then they started to climb again. Their path led beside beautiful waterfalls coming down from the mountain snows.

"I think I see the footbridge!" Justin yelled. "Down there over the creek."

"You are right! We got up here fast! You are good hikers!" Kurt told the group.

The kids ran the last part of the trail to the footbridge. Then they started searching for the clue.

"Mrs. X never wants these to be too easy," Juan said. "We're going to have to work!"

First they looked under the handrails. Then

they looked under the bridge. Still no clue!

"There's just one more place to try," Justin said. "Under one of those big stones at the end of the bridge."

Sure enough, the white edge of an envelope peeked out from under the stone. Juan pulled it out and quickly opened it.

"O.K. Here's our clue." He read:

Look for a sign at the top of this hill,

Schönbielhütte (Shun-beel-hut) *the sign*

says and points the way.

Locate the hut at the end of your climb,

You'll get a surprise at the end of the day!

CHAPTER 6

Mountain Surprises!

"There it is – the *Schönbielhütte* sign!" Kurt said. "We are almost there!"

They looked out towards a small stone house that sat alone on a cliff. The huge high mountains all around made it look tiny.

"It's a real house!" said Lisa.

"You didn't believe me," laughed Kurt.

"It's like the top of the world here! See how close the Matterhorn looks, kids! As if you could touch it," said Miss Lake.

"Many climbers stop at my grandfather's hut," Kurt said. "It is the last one on the way to the top."

"I'm glad *we're* not going to the top today," laughed Justin. "That last climb was hard. I'm ready for the hut. And more fondue!"

"Tonight will be your turn to drop your bread!" Amy said.

"No way!" laughed Justin. "I saw what Juan had to do!"

"Let's get to the hut," said Lisa. "I want to see what it's like inside. And I want to meet Kurt's grandfather!"

They set off quickly for the hut. Soon they could see a person walking towards them. Kurt started waving. "It is Grandfather! He is coming to meet us!"

Soon the older man was hugging his grandson happily. He had snow-white hair and skin tanned from high mountain days.

"Welcome to the *Schönbielhütte!*" he said. "I have been waiting and watching for you! Did my Kurt take good care of you?"

"Oh, yes! " they all said together.

"This is my grandfather Rolf," Kurt said. "Now tell him all your names!" Rolf smiled warmly as he listened.

"Come down to the hut," he told them. "I've got some cider for you. We can sit out on the porch and watch the alpenglow. That is when the sun goes down and the mountain have a magical pink color."

They all hiked on down to the hut.

"When will we find out what the surprise is?" Amy asked.

"Soon! It has to get dark first," Kurt said and smiled.

Soon they were all on the porch looking out over the mountains. The sun was slowly going down, and the snow looked pink and gold.

"How many times have you climbed the Matterhorn, sir?" Juan asked Rolf.

"Nine times. When I go with Kurt that will be the tenth. And the best!" he said. "Kurt is ready. He will be a great mountain climber!"

"I only hope to be as good as you are," Kurt told his grandfather.

The darkness was slowly coming on now. The Matterhorn stood out black against the sky.

"Hey! I see a fire down there in the valley!" Amy said. "And there's another one over on that side. They look like bonfires!"

"They are! It is August 1st – our national holiday! We celebrate the beginning of the Swiss Federation," said Kurt. "All the mountain farmers light bonfires tonight. Soon the whole valley will be filled with them."

"It's like our Fourth of July," Amy said. "We have fireworks, but no bonfires."

Suddenly the sky was filled with an

explosion of color. "We have fireworks, too!" Rolf said. "Zermatt is putting on a show tonight and we can see it all from up here. Surprise!"

"Wow! This is fantastic!" Justin said. "Fireworks on top of the world. What a great surprise! Mrs. X timed this perfectly!"

"We worked hard to fix it so you would be up here for tonight," Kurt said. "And there is one more surprise to come!"

"What? What?" the kids wanted to know.

"I think you'll find an envelope under the table," Rolf said.

Amy reached down and found a tiny white envelope taped there. She started to read:

You like to ski – I'm sure you do!

And so it's been arranged for you.

Kurt will guide you – so worry not.

Your skiis are waiting at the spot.

The kids all started talking at once. "Skiing in the summer! Wow!"

"They have skiis for us!"

"What a super surprise!"

"This has been a really perfect day!" Amy told Miss Lake as they all sat there on the porch. "I want to remember every second of it. Mrs. X is going to get a super-long postcard from here!"

The fireworks kept exploding down in the valley below. And now all the mountain meadows were filled with bright bonfires.

44